Contents

Foreword

The technique used to utter a word is quite simple. Your lungs provide the energy for your vocal chords to produce sound into the trachea, the larynx then takes over, before the resonator tract turns vocal fold vibration into a word. A simple process, but one we have afforded great power to as human civilisation has evolved. Notions of respect seem paramount in modern society, and there is one word that sits at the bottom of any obscenity pile, a word widely acknowledged as the most offensive and taboo in the English language. That word, effortlessly made up of only four letters, is 'cunt'.

It doesn't sound like a bad word, quite the opposite. Rounded and concise, it has a nice click to start, and a sharp bite to finish. Its first recorded appearance was as an Oxford street name, in about 1230, and at that time it wasn't considered obscene, merely a word for the private parts of a female. By the late 14th century literary greats such as Chaucer were even using the word in a normal descriptive manner. It then seemed to disappear from popular use for a few centuries, its suppression led to increased notoriety, and when it reappeared in dictionaries in the late 20th century its definition was as a disparaging term for a person one dislikes or finds extremely disagreeable or stupid.

With such an open and subjective definition I felt it essential to investigate further. After employing a team of avid cuntspotters, it was reported that cunts now roam the earth with the menace and dominance of the dinosaurs some 100 million years previous. Many different breeds of cunt have so far been identified, and this book provides an A to Z of some of the most common found on Planet Earth today.

THE BIG BOOK OF CUNTS

By Robert Breeze

Copyright © 2016 Robert Breeze

Aggressicunt

THE AGGRESSIVE CUNT

WHERE TO SPOT THEM

PUBS   TOWN CENTRES   BETTING SHOPS

DESCRIPTION

Aggressicunts are not known for their good looks and don't tend to be physically impressive. They ordinarily lack physical stature and can be short and snappy with clenched teeth and fists. Males seem to favour polo shirts and jeans, though sometimes rip their clothes off in order to duel.

DISTRIBUTION

Aggressicunts are thought to have originated hundreds of thousands of years ago, from the onset of man as we know it. Capitalist societies now seem to breed a high proportion, notably aggressicunts who ply their trade in a non-physical manner.

LIFE SPAN

Aggressicunts have a short life span. Their aggressive nature and high alcohol intake can lead to high blood pressure or increased strain on the heart. Their main natural predator appears to be their fellow aggressicunt, and they regularly cross swords with others from their own breed.

SUB-BREEDS

**Abusicunt   Barbaricunt   Bullicunt
Destructicunt   Moronicunt**

HABITAT

Aggressicunts appear to favour environments that are packed with other males. They are fiercely territorial creatures and don't like outsiders entering into their habitat.

BEHAVIOUR

Aggressicunts lack perspective and concern themselves with petty victories. They are oversensitive and seem offended by people who stare at them. Overprotective and narrow-minded, they take life and themselves far too seriously.

DIET

The diet of these cunts seems to fuel their aggressive tendencies, and they're usually carnivores with a large red meat intake. The majority will favour alcohol over food consumption as it gives them the courage to act aggressively in as many situations as possible.

REPRODUCTION

Though aggressicunts can be aggressive towards their mating partners and offspring, they are lovers of a family unit and thus breed at a healthy rate. Their questionable parenting methods include pumping their children full of sugar then hitting them when they misbehave.

Attenticunt

THE ATTENTION SEEKING CUNT

DESCRIPTION

The attenticunt is a striking creature that regularly works on their looks. The male likes to adapt their body in order to look physically imposing, whilst the female tends to sport huge amounts of make-up. Both sexes seem to like designer clothing, but rarely miss an opportunity to flash maximum amounts of flesh.

DISTRIBUTION

Attenticunts are found almost exclusively in the developed world, and are thought to have originated in the 20th century as societies became increasingly obsessed with looks and celebrity culture. California and London seem particular breeding grounds for these cunts.

LIFE SPAN

Attenticunts live well into middle age, though their attention seeking behaviour will typically fade as their priorities change in the latter parts of their life. The celebricunt is a natural predator that will prey on the attenticunt in order to further their own careers, or in more sinister cases to satisfy their sexual urges.

HABITAT

Attenticunts can adapt quickly to new habitats, and throughout the course of a day might flit in and out of several in order to try and gain the required attention. Females seem to like surrounding themselves with homosexual males.

The female attenticunt posing

BEHAVIOUR

Attenticunts are needy, weak-minded cunts, driven by jealousy and a lack of self-worth. They always seek praise for doing good deeds and sometimes resort to goading people, a negative response deemed better than none. They often refer to themselves in the third person, and like to call themselves divas. Some are driven by an obsession with fame and celebrity and, with social media a hugely important part of their lives, they will regularly air their dirty laundry in public. They are prone to emotional statuses, and will announce to all their attendance at an event in the desperate hope that someone cares. They are audible yawners and dramatic sneezers.

DIET

The quantity and quality of the food an attenticunt consumes is geared around ensuring they conform to a desired look. For males this usually means a high food intake, for females sometimes a dangerously low one. Females in particular revel in detailing their diets on social media.

REPRODUCTION

Attenticunts tend to have children and so reproductive rates are high. Their motivations for doing so varies, but a child naturally brings more attention for the parent, and more blatant attenticunts will use their child in order to garner more attention for themselves.

SUB-BREEDS

Famehungricunt   **Insecuricunt**   **Jealousicunt**   **Munchausicunt**   **Narcissiticunt**
Selficunt   **Vainicunt**

Booricunt

THE BORING CUNT

DESCRIPTION
The booricunt is a lifeless looking critter that rarely dares to change the hairstyle given to them at a young age. Females regularly have fringes, whilst males will sport outdated centre or side partings. They are most commonly spotted in plain clothing, with traditional colours a firm favourite. V-neck jumpers, long dresses, cardigans, and orthodox underwear will often complete the look.

DISTRIBUTION
Booricunts have been around since the birth of man and are found in most communities around the world today. Their numbers are biggest in more technically developed countries such as the USA, China, Japan and the UK.

LIFE SPAN
Booricunts typically live long lives. Their predictability ensures they rarely put themselves in danger and stress levels are kept to a minimum. Anyone in their company on a regular basis will testify that their longevity seems infinite.

HABITAT
Booricunts habitually live in dull 2 up 2 down style accommodation, and are known for decorating their homes in as stale a manner as possible. When venturing outside of their regular hideout they sometimes frequent travel lodges for extended periods.

BEHAVIOUR
Booricunts are generally docile and quiet cunts. They obsess about tiredness and the quality of their sleep, and will initiate conversations about transport and the weather. They devote large parts of their time and attention towards pursuits that others see as routine, such as feeding and exercise, and regularly document both activities on social media. The only time most booricunts express notable emotion is when they encounter situations that force change to their routines, and they seem to relish ultimately pointless pursuits such as trainspotting or growing oversized vegetables.

DIET
Booricunts are monotonously repetitive when it comes to their diet. Ready meals are a particular favourite, from macaroni cheese to takeaway meals in boxes. Beans are also hugely popular.

REPRODUCTION
Booricunts are methodical breeders, often having such details as number and name of children determined from a very young age. Very few of their offspring break away from the booricunt mould, and they talk about their brood relentlessly.

SUB-BREEDS

Accounticunt   **Monoticunt**   **Routinicunt**   **Stereotypicunt**   **Trainspotticunt**

Brainwashicunt

THE BRAINWASHED CUNT

DESCRIPTION
The brainwashicunt is a weak limbed creature, usually thin with narrow minds and angular facial features. They often wear bright colours or headpieces in order to stand out in a crowd. Psychicunts, sprititualicunts, and astrologicunts like to wear mystical cloaks.

A psychicunt in action

DISTRIBUTION
Brainwashicunts are thought to have originated about two thousand years ago, with religicunts and astrologicunts amongst the first common breeds. Nowadays the biggest concentrations tend to be found in developing countries, and also in big cities with dense populations. They use this great exposure to try and convert people so they can multiply in number.

LIFE SPAN
Brainwashicunts have a below average life span dependent upon their passion. Terricunts have short life spans, sometimes taking their own life as part of their delusional dedication. Some religicunts and astrologicunts can be that obsessional they believe everything is already fated and thus lead a somewhat haphazard existence. The dictaticunt is their main natural predator and will seek to eliminate them as soon as their beliefs motivate actions seen as harmful to others.

HABITAT
Brainwashicunts traditionally live in communities, or communes, with fellow brainwashicunts.

BEHAVIOUR
Brainwashicunts will prey on the emotionally weak, unstable, or vulnerable. They trust their instincts to baffling levels and seem to love fantasy and make believe. Though brainwashicunts are largely passive creatures, terricunts are amongst the most aggressive cunts on the planet. Religicunts are bewildering brainwashicunts who believe there's an invisible man in the sky and a list of ten things that we should and shouldn't do.

DIET
Brainwashicunts feed whenever their brainwashing allows and are usually poor eaters, favouring home grown produce and recyclable foods and materials.

REPRODUCTION
Brainwashicunts are not prolific breeders, trying to increase their numbers using methods of persuasion rather than mating.

SUB-BREEDS

Aromathericunt   Astrologicunt   Fanaticunt   Fortunetellicunt   Indoctrinaticunt
Psychicunt   Religicunt   Supersticicunt   Tarotcunt   Terricunt

Capicunt

THE CAPITALIST CUNT

DESCRIPTION

The capicunt is a slick biped that usually exhibits a modern look. Most are characterised by practical hairstyles, brittle features, and an indestructible backbone. Males will wear immaculately pressed suits, relentlessly shined shoes, and are great experimenters with facial hair. Females sport cutting-edged fashions and designer accessories.

DISTRIBUTION

Though Capicunts are a phenomenon mainly spawn out of 19th and 20th century industrialisation, their origin can be traced back to early forms of merchant capitalism practiced in Western Europe during the Middle Ages. Nowadays huge swathes are found in the USA, UK, China and Japan.

LIFE SPAN

Capicunts are largely youthful creatures who put lots of pressure on themselves to achieve. The added strain means they suffer from extreme stress, and heart attacks are common. Suicide rates are also higher than average as their egos don't handle failure well. Their main natural predator is their fellow capicunt, who thinks nothing of trampling on one of their own in order to earn more money or get more power.

SUB-BREEDS

Advertisicunt	Apprenticunt
Aspiraticunt	Backstabbicunt
Bankicunt	Commuticunt
Contactlesscunt	Economisticunt
Goldiggicunt	Jargonicunt
Marketicunt	Networkicunt
Publicrelaticunt	Recruiticunt
Salesmanicunt	Starbucunt

HABITAT

Capicunts love everything modern and thus can be identified through apartments and penthouses loaded full of modern furniture and gadgets.

BEHAVIOUR

Capicunts are highly motivated cunts, often arrogant and full of their own self-importance. Though most are outwardly noisy, they are usually insecure and emotionally shallow, quick to wallow in self-pity if they think they are underachieving in life. Full of objectives and goals, when afforded positions of power they routinely belittle people they perceive to be beneath them. Young males tend to be swaggering and cock-sure, whilst females can be nasty, crafty, vindictive, and jealous, and seem largely to hate other females.

DIET

Capicunts rarely eat well, their non-stop lifestyle not conducive to a healthy balanced diet. They dine out at restaurants and are always first in the queue to try experimental new food. To supplement their food intakes, they regularly sip energy drinks and coffee on public transport.

REPRODUCTION

Capicunts are notoriously poor breeders, seemingly too concerned with their appearance and career than to reproduce. Numbers instead increase as a product of increasingly shallow societies underpinned by the notion that sex sells.

A cluster of capicunts trying to get creative at a meeting

The commuticunt manipulating a situation they deem unsatisfactory

Celebricunt

THE CELEBRITY CUNT

WHERE TO SPOT THEM

TV   CARIBBEAN ISLANDS   REHAB

NEWLY OPENED RESTAURANTS

DESCRIPTION

The celebricunt is an altered beast, spending most of its time changing appearance to try and stave off the threat of ageing. A lot are orange with protruding mouths, and they seem to like adding signature pieces to their look such as hats, gloves, or even plasters.

The protruding lips of a celebricunt

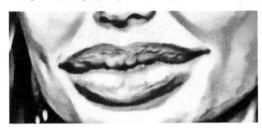

DISTRIBUTION

Celebricunts originated in the 20th century, with the USA and the UK at the forefront of their evolution. They are one of the fastest growing cunts in the world today and are increasingly spotted elsewhere in the developed and developing world, often living in clusters.

LIFE SPAN

Celebricunts are afforded access to the best healthcare and ordinarily live long lives. Despite that some are unable to resist the temptations that their lifestyles afford them, with addiction and suicide rates higher than average. They are also susceptible to being scapegoated by a politicunt, who have been known to hound these cunts out of their habitats and return them to a normal life.

HABITAT

Celebricunts primarily live in huge houses with swimming pools in major cities or luxurious retreats. Most will work on location for their jobs so their habitats vary.

BEHAVIOUR

Celebricunts are often loud, childish, and suck on the teet of fame like a thirsty piglet, desperate not to go back to former anonymity. Mentally fragile and never far from an emotional blowout, these cuntish mammalians will sell themselves in whatever manner they can, and will advertise anything to try and gain exposure. Full of their own self-importance, most are notoriously easy to tease.

DIET

Celebricunts are feeble feeders who regularly diet in order to succumb to pressure from the media and public. Some develop eating disorders, and it's rare to find a celebricunt who doesn't plan their food intake meticulously.

REPRODUCTION

Celebricunts can be calculating breeders. They will usually try and seek out a fellow celebricunt to breed with in order to further their showbiz careers, rejecting their old partners in order to do so. Increasingly it's fashionable for a celebricunt to hoard children from African nations instead of reproducing themselves.

SUB-BREEDS

Idolicunt   Mercenaricunt   Nepotismisticunt   Realicunt

Chavicunt

THE CHAV CUNT

WHERE TO SPOT THEM

OFF LICENCES   FAST FOOD SHOPS

BUS STATIONS   PASTRY SHOPS

DESCRIPTION
The chavicunt has a unique look. It is one characterised by marks on their face that originate from scars, spots, or hickies. Males usually have their hair meticulously gelled, whilst females scrape it back into a high tight ponytail. The male loves a gold sovereign ring or earring, and favours jeans and a stripy shirt as evening wear. The female likes a prominent breast tattoo and a top with a sexual slogan or the word 'bitch' on it. Both sexes sport tracksuits, caps, white socks and trainers, and can often be spotted with cigarettes lodged behind their ears.

DISTRIBUTION
Chavicunts are a UK phenomenon that originated in the early 21st century, and are found at large in highly urbanised areas.

LIFE SPAN
The chavicunt is a youthful cunt and very few get to old age. They live on average 20 years less than other cunts due to their diet and lifestyle, with prolific alcohol and nicotine intakes. Their main natural predators all tend to be authority figures, who may try to remove their habitat or even legislate against what they're allowed to wear.

A flock of chavicunts perched on a railing

HABITAT
The main habitat of the chavicunt is in flats on council estates. They occasionally venture further afield and will hang out in high towns in congregations known as groups or crews. At night they change their habitats and often gather at predetermined locations to show off their cars.

BEHAVIOUR
Chavicunts are noisy, aggressive, sarcastic, anti-social beasts. They can be friendly but act on impulse and have a short fuse, lit by anything deemed as disrespectful. Few chavicunts have jobs, but they are reasonably financially savvy and claim benefits off the state where possible.

DIET
Chavicunts feed mostly on snack food such as crisps and chocolate. Takeaways and processed meats are also popular.

REPRODUCTION
Chavicunts are incredibly fertile breeders, which helps counter-balance their low life span and regular interruptions to their breeding cycles through diseases such as Herpes or Chlamydia. When their offspring appears they can be inattentive parents who rarely stick around to raise their children into adulthood - as a result most chavicunts have either none or two dads. They tend to hunt for a mate late at night.

SUB-BREEDS

Boyracicunt   **Gobbicunt**
Hoodicunt   **Pramicunt**   **Touticunt**
Towncenticunt

Cheesicunt

THE CHEESY CUNT

WHERE TO SPOT THEM

CLAPPING   CHEERING   CHATTING

HOLIDAY REPPING   DANCING TO POP

DESCRIPTION

The cheesicunt is a sickly creature that loves grinning, seemingly with too many brilliant white teeth for their mouths. This shampooed, clean-cut cunt often gives the impression that they wash their hair and shave numerous times a day. They love slogan t-shirts and fancy dress, always taking the opportunity to try and display how wacky they are by the clothes that they wear.

DISTRIBUTION

Cheesicunts are thought to have originated in the 20th century and are now the dominant form of cunt in the USA. Here they will wish you a good day in the most dramatic manner possible.

LIFE SPAN

Though some cheesicunts cease to be in middle age due to the hard knocks life can dish out, they are clean living and the majority live for a long time. They can be susceptible to attacks from aggressicunts at odds with their chirpy nature.

HABITAT

Cheesicunts are great mother lovers and rarely leave their mother's bosom until absolutely necessary. When they do break free and leave their maternal habitat they rarely venture far and will regularly return to their home comforts.

SUB-BREEDS

Boybandicunt   Chirpicunt
Clubrepicunt   Henicunt   Lolcunt
Popmusicunt   Stagicunt
Wackicunt   Yolocunt

The wacky pose of a cheesicunt

BEHAVIOUR

Chirpy and obsessed with making people laugh, these cunts are always talking. They are typically mild mannered and try to portray a wacky persona at all times. Though kind hearted, they also tend to be conformists, with insincerity and dishonesty part of their make up. These cunts hate to offend and will choose their language carefully, sometimes overheard substituting swear words for more friendly terms such as 'pants'. They also use multiple emoticons, and often seek to be funny when naming a wi-fi network or creating home answerphone messages. They are shallow-thinkers and useless in a crisis, simply telling others to 'cheer up' when they are down.

DIET

Cheesicunts routinely have a balanced diet as they are very alert to the latest nutritional advice, almost scared to rebel towards anything with excess fat content. The only drug their systems can cope with is coffee.

REPRODUCTION

Cheesicunts find everything about children cute and thus usually seek out a mate at an early age in order to reproduce and start building towards an identikit large family. They will describe the inevitable result of unprotected lovemaking as 'incredible gifts'. Their offspring seem to develop cheesicunt atrributes early in life, with the young cheesicunt a feeble creature seemingly in need of someone to idolise.

Cheesicunts on a night out

Cowardicunt

THE COWARDLY CUNT

DESCRIPTION
The cowardicunt comes in all shapes and sizes. Routinely shy, some sport red cheeks on a regular basis.

DISTRIBUTION
The cowardicunt is a fairly modern but fast growing cunt, now found in all countries across the globe. They ordinarily form in clusters, seeking to obtain courage from being part of a group or gang. Increasingly they now originate online, that environment providing the perfect haven for them to be anonymously cuntish.

LIFE SPAN
Cowardicunts are lifelong cunts that live for long periods. The very nature of their being ensures they rarely place themselves in situations that would present tangible danger.

HABITAT
Cowardicunts usually favour tiny dwellings in areas perceived to be safe, rather than larger houses in less secure neighbourhoods. These cunts will adorn their habitat with copies of cowardly newspapers that prey on their fear.

BEHAVIOUR
Cowardicunts avoid conflict in the flesh and initially seem polite and shy. They seem scared of everything, from people they're suspicious of, to social situations, to germ, dirt, diseases, terrorists or overseas dictators. They frequently shy away from the truth, will let others take the blame, and will say what they think you want to hear rather than risk someone's disapproval. As

soon as they feel secure in an environment, or are afforded positions of power, they often abuse that position and rule by being aggressive towards others. This is rarely face-to-face, dealing with situations of potential conflict by phoning, emailing, or even leaving notes for the apple of their ire.

A cowardicunt makes threats from a distance

DIET
Cowardicunts have little or no courage and will often seek to consume things to make them feel brave. They can be great consumers of alcohol and other drugs that give them false courage.

REPRODUCTION
Cowardicunts are sometimes characterised by small genitalia, with male cowardicunts particularly lacking in the testicular department. Despite that, and the fact they are reluctant to experience real love, they keep their numbers high, seeing a large family base as a secure place from which to wield their brand of cuntishness onto society.

SUB-BREEDS

**Animalcruelticunt   Cyberbullicunt
Knificunt   Matadoricunt
Stalkericunt   Trophyhunticunt**

Cybercunt

THE CYBER CUNT

DESCRIPTION

The cybercunt is a squalid creature with notoriously poor eyesight. Hunched over due to hours spent sat in a swivel chair, this cunt can be stunted and malformed due to a lack of vitamin D caused by their indoor lifestyles. They can be recognisable through ill-fitting clothing purchased online.

DISTRIBUTION

Cybercunts originated in the late 20th century. They are found everywhere where internet facilities are at hand, primarily in developed countries. China, Japan, USA and the UK have the highest concentrations.

LIFE SPAN

Cybercunts have an average life span. They are always being watched and monitored by those in authority, with policicunts waiting to pounce if they produce, download or distribute illegal material. The geekicunts natural predator is the bullicunt.

A nocturnal cybercunt in their natural habitat

SUB-BREEDS

**Avataricunt   Geekicunt   Groomicunt
Intercunt   Interpaedofilicunt**

HABITAT

Cybercunts traditionally spend most of their time alone in darkened rooms with a webcam buzzing away. They usually change habitats only in the online world, embarking on chat based games whereby they can virtually move from the lounge to the bedroom if feeling a frisky. Often tech obsessed, they access the internet regularly on their phones when away from their habitats for any length of time.

BEHAVIOUR

Cybercunts are nocturnal beasts that seem to live their lives by monotonous routines guided by the web. They can develop different personas when online, with extreme cybercunts motivated to socialise by the thought of documenting their activities on social media after. Most are online attention seekers, and some abuse the anonymity the internet affords them to groom their way into illegal activity.

DIET

Cybercunts do most of their shopping online so tend to shun fresh food in favour of tinned and frozen produce. They favour quick simple meals for fear of being removed from their computers for too long.

REPRODUCTION

Cybercunts typically baulk at the thought of children, deeming them an unwelcome distraction to their virtual world. Traditionally loners, their numbers instead increase in line with technological advances. If they pair off it is usually with a fellow cybercunt, and thus they routinely conduct the majority of their relationship online.

19

Daticunt

THE DATING CUNT

DESCRIPTION

The daticunt is not traditionally an attractive creature and can be slight of stature with poor eyesight. They will often wear distinctive necker scarfs and carry accessories such as flowers in order to identify themselves to a potential partner.

DISTRIBUTION

The daticunt is a modern day phenomenon that originated in the late 20th century. They now exist in all countries throughout the world, though their methods vary greatly from region to region. In capitalist societies the drive to put work before family has seen numbers increase greatly in the last hundred years.

LIFE SPAN

Daticunts are at their most prolific when aged in their 20s and 30s and rarely get to old age. Unique cunts in that they don't have any natural predators, if they haven't ensnared a partner by their 50s most lose their spirit and give up.

HABITAT

Daticunts increasingly operate in an online habitat, and so are usually only spotted outdoors when actually on a date.

BEHAVIOUR

These cunts have bitter undertones to most of their behaviour as essentially it's frustrating to them they haven't yet acquired the partner they actively seek. They also operate in very different ways dependent on their sex. Males seem to have an air of desperation about them, whereas the female seems to thrive on the dating scene. Some females become serial daters and will meet man after man, each time citing a lack of spark before moving on to the next.

DIET

Daticunts don't have any notable dietary routines, though by the very nature of their being will eat out in restaurants and bars maybe once or twice a week. Females tend to eat better than males, as in the majority of instances the male feels obliged to purchase all the food. In an attempt to satisfy their frugal single lifestyles, the single male will then not eat as plentifully as his potential partner.

REPRODUCTION

Daticunts have lower than average reproductive rates. Some inevitably pair off and breed during their dating years, but with their life span a short one many find they miss the boat when it comes to having children.

SUB-BREEDS

Eharmicunt   Matchicunt   Serialdaticunt   Speedaticunt   Tindercunt

Dictaticunt

THE DICTATOR CUNT

DESCRIPTION

The dictaticunt is an old-fashioned looking beast, routinely male with bulging veins and a shiny forehead. They like militaristic outfits and will try to influence the masses with their look.

DISTRIBUTION

The dictaticunt is thought to have originated as a product of the Roman Empire. The modern day dictaticunt is ordinarily found in large cities and will usually rule autocracies. They seem to thrive more in areas where there are huge disparities between rich and poor, and where freedoms are hard to come by.

LIFE SPAN

Dictaticunts usually have a shorter than average life span due to the stresses, physical and mental, that they place on themselves in order to develop into a top drawer cunt. High level politicunts have been known to gang up in order to remove the dictaticunt from their habitat and eliminate their cuntish being.

HABITAT

Dictaticunts ordinarily live in huge palatial buildings, and will almost always have a room dedicated to showing off their achievements.

BEHAVIOUR

Dictaticunts are all about totalitarian control and like to publicly appear strong and confident. Largely narcissistic and lacking integrity, they can be aggressive and wild with their instructions. Despite this, the dictaticunt seems to shy away from conflict themselves, instead deploying obedient subjects or troops to carry out their actions and fight for them.

DIET

The diet of a dictaticunt is typically high in protein content. They have also been known to supplement their diet with drugs such as speed and cocaine, both of which accentuate their cuntish qualities.

REPRODUCTION

Reproductive rates amongst dictaticunts are unclear. The most abominable dictaticunts have been known to demand that their people look like them, so numbers can be hard to gauge.

SUB-BREEDS

Autocraticunt	Despoticunt	Meglomanicunt
Oligarchicunt	Totalitaricunt	Tyranticunt

A dictaticunt making sure he is heard loud and clear

Evilicunt

THE EVIL CUNT

DESCRIPTION

The evilicunt doesn't have a definitive look, coming in various forms, guises and disguises. Not being instantly recognisable is advantageous to the evilicunt as it means they can exhibit their despicable, turgid, cuntish behaviour in an underhand manner.

DISTRIBUTION

Evilicunts have been around since the birth of human civilisation. Today, the evilicunt is found almost exclusively in economically developed countries. Though nations such as Belgium and Austria occasionally unearth a phenomenally ghastly evilicunt, the USA leads the way for evilicunts per head of population, closely followed by the UK.

LIFE SPAN

The evilicunt will rarely get to old age, with constant threats to their life coming from capital punishment in countries that still adopt it, or from vigilantes in countries that don't. The politicunt, dictaticunt, and policicunt will all try to bring an evilicunt down at different stages of the judicial process, whether the intent is to rehabilitate or eliminate from society. The evilicunt is even viewed as sub-human scum by most of their fellow inmates in prison and are often attacked there.

HABITAT

Evilicunts are habitually found in prison if charged for their behaviour, the most relentless cunts in soilitary confinement. Otherwise evilicunts are great lurkers. Their favoured spots seem to be in small towns or the countryside. Some evilicunts spend lots of time in cellars or secret gardens to keep their vile habits hidden from the world.

BEHAVIOUR

The evilicunt is a repulsively complex cunt, with very little known of how their mind actually works. They are routinely aggressive, volatile, obnoxious, and socially and sexually inept. Often coming with personality disorders, they can be guarded and clinical operators, if not exceptionally violent then extremely cunning. Most have no affinity with animals.

DIET

Evilicunts are almost exclusively carnivores, feasting on anything from animal carcasses to the flesh of their victims. They love to hunt and kill their prey themselves, getting a sadistic pleasure from the whole process.

REPRODUCTION

Evilicunts are entirely selfish, tend to be loners, and thus have very low reproductive rates. If they find themselves with children they usually either disown them at an early age, or are abusive or cruel towards them.

SUB-BREEDS

Paedofilicunts   **Rapicunts**   **Serialkillericunt**   **Slavericunt**   **Trafficunt**

Evilicunts routinely take pleasure from hurting other living creatures

Fibicunt

THE LYING CUNT

DESCRIPTION
The fibicunt comes in all shapes and sizes, but usually have faces beset by wrinkles. They are great fidgeters, can develop facial ticks, and are commonly spotted with just a hint of a smile and raised eyebrows. Bald fibicunts usually wear wigs.

The fibicunt often clasps their hands and fidgets

DISTRIBUTION
Fibicunts have been around for thousands of years and are found in all countries across the world. Capitalist countries now tend to have the highest concentrations, with bullshiticunts particularly populous in these areas.

LIFE SPAN
Fibicunts typically live shorter than average lives as their existence is a stressful one. The opinionaticunt and miseraablicunt are their two main threats. Both are suspicious of the fibicunt and seem intent on questioning them to find holes in their stories. Adultericunts can often be the victim of revenge attacks when the unsuspecting partners find out.

HABITAT
Though the fibicunt doesn't seem to have any specific dwelling or area of residence, the majority have a common trait in that they will exaggerate their habitats and suggest they are nicer than they are.

BEHAVIOUR
Fibicunts can be very irritating and annoying to deal with. They are defensive, cagey cunts, who avoid eye contact and give unnecessary explanations. They meticulously plan and plot their stories, all characterised by a huge amount of bullshit. They need no rhyme or reason to lie, and most lie with a confidence and conviction that they'll never be caught.

DIET

Fibicunts will pick and nibble at food, sneaking a lot of it into them when backs are turned. Those at either end or the weight spectrum will either conceal how much or how little they are consuming.

REPRODUCTION

The reproductive rates of fibicunts are hard to gauge. Adultericunts and cheaticunts are thought to bolster the breeding rates of these cunts with their carnal activities.

SUB-BREEDS

Adultericunt   Bullshiticunt   Cheaticunt   Deceiticunt
Fabricaticunt   Sneakicunt

Greedicunt

THE GREEDY CUNT

DESCRIPTION

The greedicunt is ordinarily a round, clinically obese creature that rarely has an identifiable neck. Usually over 20 stone in weight they can appear to be boneless, but this beast is in fact just protected by layer upon layer of skin, usually hidden beneath loose-fitting creased clothing. Their look is often characterised by facial features each battling with each other to be deemed the largest on their oversized heads.

The inflated bottom of a faticunt

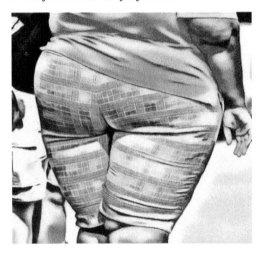

DISTRIBUTION

Greedicunts are a fairly modern phenomenon in human civilisation, as they only originate where a certain level of wealth is present. They are found almost exclusively in economically developed nations around the world, and are the fastest growing form of cunt in the UK and USA.

LIFE SPAN

Huge pressure is placed upon the hearts of greedicunts, thus they usually take their last heavy breath before pensionable age. Faticunts don't have too many direct predators, though the materialisticunt, layzicunt, and mollycoddlicunt can often provide competition for food.

HABITAT

Greedicunts adopt various habitats dependent on whether their greed is motivated by wealth or food. Faticunts seem to favour living with their mothers.

BEHAVIOUR

Greedicunts have a selfish and excessive desire for more than is needed or deserved. Faticunts can be susceptible to mood swings, jolly when well fed but withdrawn if feeding time isn't near. When hungry they can be irritable, childlike, and submissive towards anyone with food.

DIET

Greedicunts are the most abundant eaters in the world. The proverbial dustbin, they rarely bother with fruit or vegetables and instead tend to be great snackers, with crisps, chocolate and fizzy drinks forming a large part of their daily intake.

REPRODUCTION

Some greedicunts are almost asexual towards the act of reproduction, and replace such urges with more acquisitional desires. It's a safer form of satisfaction for some breeds as the faticunt is at risk of health problems when physically over-exerting themselves. Those that breed produce faticunt offspring from a young age, filling their children full of sugar at ages when they are devoid of choice.

Excessicunt   **Faticunt**   **Obesicunt**   **Potbellicunt**
Rolipolicunt   **Sweaticunt**

A Greedicunt feeding, the eyes rolling back to show maximum pleasure

Hippicunt

THE HIPPY CUNT

WHERE TO SPOT THEM

FIELDS   FESTIVALS   RAMBLING

NUDIST BEACHES   BASKETED BIKES

DESCRIPTION
The hippicunt is a limp being characterised by a wrinkled face. Males ordinarily sport beards, and both sexes will experiment with varying lengths of body hair at different points of their lives. Females like flowers, both on their clothing and as hairpieces. Baggy oversized rags and long hair hidden beneath a hat are looks favoured by both sexes, though some breeds of hippicunt are at their happiest with no clothes on as they perceive this to be at one with nature. They also like necklaces and bangles, with expired festival wristbands a modern accessory.

DISTRIBUTION
Hippicunts are a 20th century phenomenon, with the movement spawning them originating in the USA in the early 1960s. Nowadays they tend to be found largely in economically developed countries, societies that they thrive in trying to reign against.

LIFE SPAN
Hippicunts live a relatively stressfree existence which is thought to contribute to a healthy lifespan, and are often hippicunts at birth and death. Though these cunts detest organised exercise such as gymnasiums, they will instead exercise and cleanse their minds.

HABITAT
Hippicunts chiefly live in weather-beaten old houses in the countryside. Loving to be at one with nature they shun urbanisation. Inside their habitats they plump for lots of antiques, bead curtains instead of doors, and their habitat is identifiable by the stench of incense and joss sticks.

BEHAVIOUR
Hippicunts are free spirits who like to broaden their mind, with self-help books a particular favourite. They are best described as wishy-washy and some attach themselves to revolts against society or movements against the ruling class. They can be self-righteous and sanctimonious, and often lack the ability and drive to offer solutions to problems. Though they champion peace and love, they can actually be aggressive and stubborn in the face of forced organisation or obedience. They love a conspiracy theory.

DIET
Hippicunts detest genetically modified or processed food, and are usually herbivores that love nothing more than eating or smoking something that has surged out of the ground.

REPRODUCTION
Most hippicunts live off the back of the notion of free love and thus spend a lot of time on their backs trying to reproduce. The rate at which they multiply has slowed in recent years as they find it economically less viable in increasingly capitalist societies.

SUB-BREEDS

Activisticunt   **Bohemicunt**   **Festicunt**   **Naturicunt**   **Organicunt**

Two bangled hippicunts making the recognisable sign for peace in the midst of a tree

Layzicunt

THE LAZY CUNT

WHERE TO SPOT THEM

SOFAS   SOCIAL SECURITY OFFICES

UNIVERSITIES   STOOD ON ESCALATORS

DESCRIPTION

The layzicunt is an underdeveloped creature whose limbs aren't used frequently enough to fully prosper. They seem to wear clothing for comfort, with baggy jogging bottoms and dressing gowns most common.

DISTRIBUTION

Layzicunts have only really multiplied in number from the 20th century onwards. They are now found in their millions worldwide, with the more developed countries of the USA and the UK leading the way for sheer numbers.

LIFE SPAN

The lifespan of a layzicunt is higher than average. They don't exert themselves more than they have to which contributes to their longevity. Though the nature of their existence dictates they don't have to deal with many natural predators, if they make it as far as a workplace they are routinely eaten up by capicunts or aspiraticunts.

SUB-BREEDS

Middlemanagicunt   Oaficunt
Procrasticunt
Royalticunt   Studenticunt

HABITAT

Layzicunts are traditionally found hibernating on sofas or in beds, usually in the houses they were born in.

BEHAVIOUR

Layzicunts are typically docile cunts, with any physical aggression or enthusiasm deemed too wasteful. These cuntish critters are unlikely to share their emotions or compromise, and they are susceptible to being brainwashed, tending to be too lazy to question prescribed doctrines or behaviours. They spend the majority of their days sitting or sleeping.

DIET

Layzicunts live almost entirely off goods that can be consumed with minimal effort. Ready meals with utensils included are favoured as it requires minimal washing up, and they are great snackers. Most food will be consumed in the lounge area of their habitats.

REPRODUCTION

Layzicunts have a languorous attitude towards reproducing. Though they spend longer than most in bed, the thought of extended physical activity is often enough to ensure that their reproduction habits are unsubstantial.

An immobile layzicunt, barely dressed, feeding whilst lying down

Materialisticunt

THE MATERIALISTIC CUNT

DESCRIPTION

The materialisticunt comes in all shapes, sizes and forms. At a glance they are one of the hardest cunts to spot as some go as far as to alter their appearance with plastic surgery. The female is most recognisable as clothing and fashion seems to form a key part of their lives. They will research the latest fashions to try and ensure they remain on trend, and thus usually sport designer wear with flashy accessories.

DISTRIBUTION

Historically the highest concentrations of materialisticunts originate in those countries that developed first economically. As more countries across the globe are influenced by Western culture, their numbers have spread to the point that they are one of the fastest growing cunts in the world today. South East Asia and Dubai are their modern meccas.

LIFE SPAN

Materialisticunts are usually clean living cunts and thus live long lives. Most fade out of existence as they approach older age.

HABITAT

The modern day materialisticunt is a highly territorial creature that treasures their habitat. They don't like anyone entering their habitat or touching their goods without permission, and will often have locks on their doors if living in shared accommodation. They routinely adorn their habitats with modern techological devices.

SUB-BREEDS

**Consumeristicunt   Gadgetticunt
Possessicunt   Superficicunt**

Materialisticunts swarming during a sale

BEHAVIOUR

Materialisticunts are consumerists obsessed by gadgets and material goods, and most of their behaviours stem from this preoccupation. They will embrace every part of modern day society, and routinely equate things in terms of goods or money. Emotionally immature, they will hide underlying emotional issues beneath purchases of clothing and other items.

DIET

Materialisticunts aren't great feeders and don't value their food. They will eat on the go, and can be spotted at shopping malls eating pre, post, and even mid-shop at times.

REPRODUCTION

Materialisticunts are not prolific breeders, but when they do breed their offspring are mostly immersed into materialistic worlds from a young age. They will use computer games and gadgets as tools with which to occupy their children, so they can have more time concentrating on their own superficial lifestyles.

35

Mechanicunt

THE MECHANICAL CUNT

DESCRIPTION
The mechanicunt is an oily being, slightly hunched over due to hours on end spent in vehicles. Their attire is synonymous with their lifestyle and they love boiler suits, leather, and helmets. Caps bearing the name of their favourite engine manufacturer are also popular.

DISTRIBUTION
Mechanicunts originated post industrial revolution, and are now found in most industrialised countries across the world. The densest populations are in China, Japan, the USA and UK.

LIFE SPAN
Mechanicunts have a below average lifespan due to the dangerous nature of their chosen vice. Their pursuits can also have the knock on effect of shortening the life span of those around them, and of the planet in general.

SUB-BREEDS

Engineericunt   **Objectumsexualicunt**
Petrolicunt   **Revheadicunt**

HABITAT
Mechanicunts will favour outdoor habitats, and seem to spend most of their time in oily environments.

BEHAVIOUR
Mechanicunts are all about velocity. They obsess about the quickest point from A to B, modifying engines they own in order to help them achieve this goal. They are often devoid of personalities capable of interacting with others to achieve fulfilment, and some hardcore mechanicunts even experience emotional desires towards inanimate objects.

DIET
Mechanicunts view food as fuel, and thus tend to dine out mainly on calorific meats.

REPRODUCTION
Mechanicunts are notoriously selfish lovers, preferring to concentrate on pleasuring their engines rather than partners. Reproductive rates are low and it is thought that many mechanicunts have smaller than average reproductive organs.

Sometimes only the bottom half of a mechanicunt will be visible in public

Miseraablicunt

THE MISERABLE CUNT

DESCRIPTION

The miseraablicunt has a hangdog look, seemingly characterised by too much skin for their face. Often beset by wrinkles in their latter years, they usually have poor postures and frown a lot. They are great fans of the humble jumper and can be spotted wearing them in all weather. The gothicunt in particular loves wearing black.

DISTRIBUTION

The miseraablicunt is a first world phenomenon that seems to have originated in the 19th century. Most are spawned from the strains and stresses of modern capitalist societies, with France having the highest concentrations per hectare.

LIFE SPAN

Miseraablicunts have lengthy life spans. They thrive in later life, perhaps boosted by the fact that it becomes more socially acceptable to be miserable as the years go on.

SUB-BREEDS

Gothicunt   Grumpicunt
Melancholicunt
Moanicunt   Pessimisticunt

HABITAT

The majority of miseraablicunts live in sparsely decorated accommodation, often alone. Walls are typically magnolia in colour, and they struggle to see the natural beauty in gardens or plants. Unsociable creatures, they tend to be somewhat nocturnal, spending long periods alone in their bedrooms. Rarely will they adorn their surroundings with photographs.

BEHAVIOUR

Miseraablicunts rarely display any tangible emotions, especially those of joy. They don't seem to like themselves very much, yet still think they're better than the rest of the world. Lacking a sense of humour, these cunts love to pick fights and despise people who dare use emoticons or excessive punctuations in communications, most notably exclamation marks. They also live in the past and frown upon immaturity and organised fun.

DIET

Miseraablicunts usually eat healthily, rarely allowing themselves exotic or fattening comfort foods that might heighten their mood. They are creatures of habit when it comes to feeding and will monotonously make their own lunches for work.

REPRODUCTION

Reproductive rates amongst miseraablicunts aren't high, and they struggle to entangle breeding partners into their miserable lives. Instead their numbers increase when money rather than happiness begins to drive communities around the world.

A pair of miseraablicunts struggling to appreciate nature and instead contemplating the misery the future holds

Mollycoddlicunt

THE MOLLYCODDLED CUNT

DESCRIPTION
The mollycoddlicunt is a pale, sickly-looking creature that usually exhibits the hairstyle given to them by their parents. Always intent on wrapping up warm and catering for any weather eventuality, they usually wear an extra layer of clothing than is necessary and love scarves and hats. They will wield an umbrella at the first sign of drizzle, and a handkerchief on first sneeze.

DISTRIBUTION
Mollycoddlicunts have been around for thousands of years and are now found in all countries of the world. Whereas mollycoddlicunts in Europe and Asia tend to originate from those lacking perspective, mollycoddlicunts in Africa and the Middle East are often necessarily smothered from a young age in order to ensure a successful transition to adulthood.

LIFE SPAN
The mollycoddlicunt has a healthy life span, despite sometimes suffering from vitamin D deficiencies. Their nurtured being means that they are sometimes shielded from some of the dangers of modern society and stand a greater chance of living above the national average. They will sometimes fade out of existence in middle age if finally forced to stand on their own two feet.

SUB-BREEDS

Competiparenticunt   Complainicunt
Fussicunt   Hygienicunt
Hypochondricunt   Pampericunt
Spoilticunt

HABITAT
These cunts spent most of their lives indoors, with their beds central to their habitat. They rarely flee their mother's bosom until absolutely necessary.

BEHAVIOUR
Not independent and anything but assertive, mollycoddlicunts seem to lack perspective and will concern themselves with futile matters. Often bed-wetters into their teens, they develop into great complainers and throw tantrums. Most are sniffly cunts who exaggerate illness, and they are thought to be amongst the only cunts in the world aware of the concept of tog ratings on duvets.

DIET
The mollycoddlicunt is a feeble feeder and spends large parts of their lives in fear of, or in grip of, numerous allergies. They will stick to classic food groups and rarely experiment. They religiously observe use by dates on food and drink, and will throw dairy produce out the second their nostrils deem it to be on the turn.

REPRODUCTION
Mollycoddlicunts don't favour reproduction at any great rate as it causes considerable upset to their lives and routines. More than any other breed of cunt they are a product of the behaviour of others, and seem powerless to stop the process of overprotective, pushy parents trying to validate themselves through the achievements of their children.

A mollycoddlicunt on their way to work

Opinionaticunt

THE OPINIONATED CUNT

DESCRIPTION
The opinionaticunt is a stubborn pasty-looking creature that tends to be in physically poor shape.

DISTRIBUTION
Opinionaticunts originate mostly in capitalist countries around the world. Access to a certain level of education and computer systems seems key in the development of these cunts.

LIFE SPAN
Opinionaticunts have an average lifespan, with their later years often characterised by bitterness towards modern generations and the world they live in.

HABITAT
The modern day opinionaticunt spends the majority of their time indoors. The online habitat has become the perfect forum from which to spout their largely negative views, and provides a safe haven from which they force their opinions onto others.

A rare cross breed, the papatrollicunt

BEHAVIOUR
The opinionaticunt consistently feels the need to comment and offer opinion. They will plagiarise others and if questioned can become insecure and defensive, with their whole being seemingly fuelled by a want to appear intelligent. They seem to thrive off the attention that writing a few negative words can bring and love arguing on internet forums; such behaviour producing the newly discovered trollicunt. They are active on social media, often signing off their antagonistic ramblings with statements like 'that is all'.

DIET
Opinionaticunts don't need much food to sustain their existence. The opportunity to incite debate seems to act like a kind of fuel for most of these cunts, and food and drink are secondary necessities to the primary act of giving their views on a subject.

REPRODUCTION
Opinionaticunts aren't sociable cunts and thus their reproductive rates aren't high. Typically unattractive and bitter, they can struggle to attract partners into their midst.

SUB-BREEDS

**Antagonisticunt   Bloggicunt
Journalisticunt   Paparazzicunt
Reviewicunt   Trollicunt
Tedtalkicunt**

Patricunt

THE PATRIOTIC CUNT

DESCRIPTION
The patricunt is a thick set beast whose appearance fits the traditional look of the country where they live. They tend to dress smartly and love a dress code. Military uniforms are a favourite, and medals, flag pins, and even commemorative war watches, can complete the look.

DISTRIBUTION
Patricunts have been around for thousands of years, since settlements were first formed. Ruling classes have historically understood the importance of upholding traditions and heritages in order to safeguard their interests or empires. They form a strong national identity that spawns millions of patricunts, some of which go on to fight for their country and interests.

LIFE SPAN
Patricunts have below average life spans and are lifelong cunts whose patriotic tendencies become stronger as they get older. Their main natural predators seem to come from within their own breed, with thousands killed when patricunts from different nations fight fiercely to protect the land their country inherits.

HABITAT
Patricunts will adorn their homes and cars with national flags during times of heightened national fever. They quickly become attached to their habitats and rarely move, seeing it as a hugely laudable quality to remain close to their roots.

SUB-BREEDS

Communitaricunt   Militaricunt
Nationalisticunt   Traditionalicunt

A patricunt cherishing a piece of fabric

BEHAVIOUR
Loyal and conservative, patricunts are suspicious of those who come from different places to themselves, often to the point of regions within their own country. Not great thinkers, they can be confused beings full of hypocrisy. They will claim to be pro-life, when in fact they are anti-woman, and struggle to understand the difference between backing their country and their government. Conformists who tend not to question, they are obsessed by immigration and the actions of minorities.

DIET
Patricunts aren't experimental feeders and will largely stick to tried and tested traditional dishes.

REPRODUCTION
Though they don't seem to really like women, the male patricunt is a prolific breeder, seeing it as their duty to reproduce and keep numbers of their own strong. They will try and mould their children into patricunts, bleating on about the heritage of their country and importance of being patriotic. It helps keep their numbers constant in the face of the threat posed by increasingly multi-cultural societies

Politicunt

THE POLITICAL CUNT

DESCRIPTION
The politicunt is a spineless, gutless, physically feeble creature. They are one of the more bizarre looking cunts, often with shiny lopsided hair that looks as though it's been steamed on. Whilst professionally they are rarely out of a suit, socially they are advised on what to wear in order to make themselves more electable. Thus they like to be seen to be up to date with modern fashion or wear the colours of a particular cause they're trying to champion.

DISTRIBUTION
Politicunts originated in most countries from about the 16th century onwards, and now are found mostly in major cities throughout the world. There will usually be at least one in every town and city across the globe, wherever there is a constituency to represent.

LIFE SPAN
The politicunt lives a long, prosperous life. Their main natural predators are the opinionaticunt or activisticunt, who possess the power to bring a politicunt down when working together in large groups.

HABITAT
Politicunts live in leafy accommodation and routinely have more than one place of residence. They will inhabit grand old buildings in the centre of cities for their work, and then either stay in hotels or countryside retreats for the rest of their time.

BEHAVIOUR
Politicunts are renowned for being liars and hypocrites. Manipulative and devious, they are not to be trusted and are more concerned with winning favour than maintaining principles. They are adaptable, flexible creatures, a quality they display when regularly crawling up people's backsides to facilitate movement into positions of power.

DIET
Politicunts are routinely traditional when it comes to their diet, using their food as a way of showing their patriotism without being deemed politically incorrect.

REPRODUCTION
Politicunts are competent breeders, often bred directly from other politicunts. They seem to deduce from early in their careers that establishing a firm family based existence is key to attracting the family voter. They tend to produce unhappy children, with political correctness and bureaucratic red tape thought to stifle happy childhoods.

SUB-BREEDS

Conservicunt	Constituticunt
Corrupticunt	Democraticunt
Governmenticunt	Hypocriticunt
Leftwingicunt	Liberalicunt
Ministericunt	Politicorrecticunt
Republicunt	Rightwingicunt
Thatchicunt	

Poshicunt

THE POSH CUNT

DESCRIPTION
The poshicunt comes in 2 forms, both recognisable for their floppy hair and smooth complexion. The more dominant form of the breed is broad shouldered and adapt their bodies to suit sports such as rowing and rugby. They are usually spotted either topless or with a rugby shirt on, collar turned up. Chino style shorts, designer underwear and loafers or leather sandals complete the look. The frailer form of the breed has an upturned nose, thin facial features, and a strained voice. They rarely remove their woollen blazers or ties, and tweed is a favoured fabric. The female poshicunt tends to dress traditionally in long expensive flowing dresses.

DISTRIBUTION
Poshicunts originated from aristocracies throughout the western world and are thought to have been here for hundreds of years. They usually form in clusters alongside other poshicunts in leafy neighbourhoods, more prominently in the countryside than in urban areas.

A cluster of poshicunts trying to find a defenceless being to kill

LIFE SPAN
Poshicunts live long lives, having access to the best lifestyles and medical care, and will sometime use butlers or servants to help lighten their physical loads. Due to their wealth and status the majority live their lives in fear only of high ranking capicunts, politicunts, or aggressicunts.

HABITAT
In childhood the poshicunt will often reside in private and boarding schools. When older, they traditionally live in large detached houses with various outbuildings.

BEHAVIOUR
Poshicunts like to portray an airy, laid back, relaxed, persona to the world, but underneath are usually anxious individuals who can fret about land and inheritance issues. Females can be highly manipulative.

DIET
Poshicunts are prolific carnivores and love nothing more than to feel macho by executing the whole process themselves. Their ideal catch would be something you could hunt, catch, gut, pluck and then eat. Caviar and sushi are also particular favourites.

REPRODUCTION
Poshicunts are notoriously selfish lovers which can lead to slower than expected reproductive rates. Inbreeding has long been suspected.

SUB-BREEDS

Barristericunt   Foxhunticunt
Polocunt   Regatticunt

45

Prejudissicunt

THE PREJUDICED CUNT

DESCRIPTION

The prejudissicunt has a broad spectrum of forms, but is most commonly overweight with beady eyes, droopy faces and oversized ears. Though they historically like uniforms, the modern day breed seems to love nothing more than showing off their chubby naked torso complete with tattoos depicting symbols or literature akin to their allegiance. Racisticunts occasionally wear white gowns.

A young redneckicunt

DISTRIBUTION

Prejudissicunts are historically most associated with Germany and Austria in the 20th century, through a Nazi ideology involving the death and torture of millions of innocent Jewish people. Though most prominent in the developing world, in the UK and USA prejudissicunts tend to originate in small towns and settlements where people aren't used to other cultures and personalities.

SUB-BREEDS

Judgmenticunt	**Homophobicunt**
Nazicunt	**Racisticunt**
Redneckicunt	**Sexisticunt**

LIFE SPAN

In most countries of the developed world the behaviour of prejudissicunts is deemed unacceptable and legislation is adopted with the aim of ending their existence. Thus they have shorter than average lifespans and the politicunt is their main natural predator. Those who get through to old age become titanic prejudissicunts towards the end of their lives.

HABITAT

Prejudissicunts historically spent a lot of time in hideouts such as bunkers, but the modern day creature usually lives in simple accommodation in small towns and villages. In the USA they favour ranches.

BEHAVIOUR

Prejudissicunts are generally insecure and their behaviour seems to be motivated by a fear of those different to themselves. The vicious adrenalized hatred and discrimination that spits out of them when venting their fury is tempered by a more placid approach towards those considered to be of similar backgrounds.

DIET

Prejudissicunts are mainly carnivorous beasts that attach themselves to food befitting of the culture they were born into. Often the more flavour an ingredient has the more it is viewed with suspicion. Extreme racisticunts don't see the irony in gleefully eating food that originates from nations they otherwise hate on.

REPRODUCTION

Prejudissicunts can be productive breeders. They see it as their responsibility to try and get as many 'of their own' into the world as possible.

Pretenticunt

THE PRETENTIOUS CUNT

DESCRIPTION

The pretenticunt is a showy creature, typically with high cheekbones. Males are usually unattractive, and regularly choose to cover most of their face with hair. They will also fight baldness to the bitter end. Females favour dresses and can often be spotted sporting the latest hairstyles.

DISTRIBUTION

Prententicunts were almost exclusively born out of more opulent areas of the globe in the 20th century, only found where basic provisions are readily met. These circumstances allow them to concentrate on spurious displays of interest in other areas, typically culturally rich or artistic circles. They tend to form in great clusters, with East London in the UK and Los Angeles in the USA notable meccas.

LIFE SPAN

Pretenticunts are thought to have a longer than average lifespan, as they historically only originate where they have comfortable lifestyles.

HABITAT

Prententicunts love artistic arenas and are loathe to be seen at commercially successful events. Instead they spend a lot of their time trying to find niche habitats of artistic merit to try and fawn over. Increasingly, pretenticunts will compete with chavicunts for run down habitats in inner city areas, keen to tell all about the edgy character and hidden beauty of their new territory.

BEHAVIOUR

Pretenticunts often lack talent and thus will overstate their values, opinions, and general importance. They tend to be snobs and anything they perceive to be beneath them will be pitied and ridiculed. They will tell you how many languages they speak before exchanging basic introductory pleasantries, and start conversations only so they can then steer the subject back to themselves. They appear obsessed by appearing recondite and didactic at all times, and will gleefully refer to themselves as both.

DIET

Pretenticunts are obsessed by food and drink, and will turn their noses up at any item that comes out of a can or carton. Fish and wine are their favoured produce, with the high end of each product allowing ample opportunity for the prenticunt to preen and offer opinion. They seem to take an obscure interest in what the animal they are about to eat has been fed, and thus end up eating concotions such as grass-fed beef.

REPRODUCTION

Whilst the orgasm of a pretenticunt can often be heard from several blocks away, they are in fact fairly mediocre breeders. Those that do breed ensure numbers remain constant by moulding their children into pretenticunts from a very young age. Typically they read, drink coffee, and play musical instruments earlier than their peers.

SUB-BREEDS

Articunt   **Hipstericunt**   **Primadonnicunt**   **Snobbicunt**

The pretenticunt will claim to appreciate beauty others can't see

Randicunt

THE RANDY CUNT

DESCRIPTION
The randicunt is a slippery creature. Predominantly male, some have one arm bigger than the other. Most have a steely-eyed glare and make unnecessarily intense eye contact, often from behind tinted glasses. In public, they tend to dress casually, favouring clothing that is easily accessible and removable. In private some slip into their partners clothes when left alone in their habitat. Males will also sport rich coloured robes, hi-viz vests, thongs, and mankinis. Leather, handcuffs, and whips are worn by extreme randicunts.

DISTRIBUTION
Randicunts are one of the oldest forms of cunt, having originated from the very start of human civilisation. They seem to thrive more in sunny climes, with Italy believed to have the highest concentration. Increasingly, western randicunts can be found on islands throughout South-East Asia with partners far younger than them.

LIFE SPAN
Randicunts can live long fruitful lives, carnal pleasures a healthy pursuit. The daticunt is a natural predator as a randicunt in a relationship can be controlled.

HABITAT
Randicunts usually live in houses adapted to facilitate their vice. Webcams are a must and curtains often remain closed so as not to expose their kinky antics to the world.

SUB-BREEDS

**Kinkicunt   Opportunirandicunt
Pervicunt   Seedicunt   Sleazicunt
Teenicunt   Doggicunt**

A randicunt playing with himself in his habitat

BEHAVIOUR
Randicunts are sly creatures, often ashamed of their cock-fuelled activities. Unable to control their urges, they will keep their behaviour hidden from even their partners. Some are adaptable and engage in roleplay, whilst others are unimaginative and merely lunge when their urges take hold. The male seems more outspoken than the female and regularly cracks jokes with sexual undertones to them. Both sexes like the phrase 'I don't bite unless you want me to'.

DIET
Randicunts are manipulative feeders rather than prolific eaters. They will corner a sought after target and ply them with aphrodisiac foods such as caviar, oysters and ginger. Some use drugs such as rhohypnol to ensnare their prey.

REPRODUCTION
Despite the fact that foreplay will often involve applying or inserting accessories or apparatus, randicunts reproduce copiously. The sheer volume of sexual conquests ensures a high rate of unplanned offspring, though such pursuits can be curtailed by acquiring various sexually transmitted diseases.

Scabbicunt

THE SCABBY CUNT

DESCRIPTION
The scabbicunt is a flimsy, narrow cunt. They often sport a unique look with most of their clothing old and ill-fitting, whilst some cut their own hair.

DISTRIBUTION
The distribution of the scabbicunt is closely linked to economic development, thus they are thought to have first originated in the 19th century. Today, they are found mostly in urban areas in the developed world - the more money they have the more they are driven to bank as much of it as possible.

LIFE SPAN
Scabbicunts ordinarily live well into old age, maybe motivated by the discounts over 65s are afforded in today's society. Receiving their pension, though a focal target in the life of a scabbicunt, rarely signals a change of attitude towards money.

HABITAT
Historically, scabbicunts live in budget accommodation with furniture and decorations acquired for next to nothing. They usually settle in one house early and get to work on the all-consuming goal of paying off their mortgage.

BEHAVIOUR
Scabbicunts are generally quiet and composed cunts, with rare displays of adrenalin saved for pursuits such as haggling. They do not draw attention to themselves as being the last to be noticed at places can sometimes lead to them evading fees or inspectors. Their lives are governed by stifling routines designed to make their being as thrifty as possible. They will turn switches off religiously, and rarely throw anything out without first trying to sell it.

DIET
Scabbicunts are poor but creative eaters. It's not uncommon for them to create a week's worth of food in one sitting, which they pick at throughout the week whenever hungry. Tinned food, bread, rice and pasta are great fillers popular for their durability.

REPRODUCTION
Scabbicunts tend not to have high reproductive rates because of the well-documented cost of raising children. They are very aware that leading a solitary existence is the easiest and most frugal way to manage their finances.

SUB-BREEDS

Bargainhunticunt   **Economicunt**   **Frugalicunt**   **Stingicunt**   **Tighticunt**

Bargainhunticunts congregating at a car boot sale

Sporticunt

THE SPORTY CUNT

DESCRIPTION

The sporticunt comes in many forms. Whilst some are towering ox-like creatures with no discernable neck, others are thin and frail. The larger form love wearing ill-fitting tight tops so that their muscles have no choice but to bulge out of them. Shorts are considered an all-year-round garment.

DISTRIBUTION

Though the sporticunt probably originated from medieval sports in the middle ages, they have now multiplied to the point that they are some of the most common cunts found in the world today. Every settlement on the planet seems awash with them, the highest concentrations thought to be in Australia.

LIFE SPAN

Whilst some sporticunts over exert themselves and place too much strain on their organs, the majority are fit and this contributes to a lengthy life span. They cease to be usually a few years before their death, with their bodies no longer capable of taking the physical strain.

SUB-BREEDS

Cyclicunt   Exerciseaddicticunt
Gymnasicunt   Joggicunt

HABITAT

The main habitat of a sporticunt is inside stadiums and arenas purpose built for their chosen sport. Some sporticunts have their habitats modified to adapt to their lifestyles, packing them full of equipment designed to reshape their bodies.

BEHAVIOUR

On the whole the sporticunt is mild mannered, despite the fact that they often adapt their bodies into fighting machines. Most are obsessional about their chosen sport and push themselves to the brink of exhaustion.

DIET

Sporticunts are prolific feeders. Almost exclusively carnivores, these cunts are all about calorie counting and need gargantuan calorific intakes to fuel their daily lives. Some use protein shakes, energy drinks, and steroids as supplements, and refer to food as 'carbs'.

REPRODUCTION

Sporticunts are able reproducers. With many deeming themselves great lovers, they almost see it as a challenge to produce offspring and encourage their children to follow in their paths from a young age. Those sporticunts that turn to steroid use to increase or maintain their build don't fare as well, with their penises often becoming almost undetectable.

Thefticunt

THE THIEVING CUNT

DESCRIPTION

Whereas the thefticunt historically wore masks and tops with black and white stripes, the modern day thefticunt is all about headwear. From the humble baseball cap to balaclavas, all their clothing is designed to mask their true appearance. When unmasked they are almost always ugly beasts, typically with an unkempt facial appearance and bad teeth. They are fast, nippy creatures, characteristics thought to have evolved to allow quick getaways from all manner of dicey situations.

DISTRIBUTION

Thefticunts are a fairly modern phenomenon born out of developing societies around the world. When a country becomes more economically developed it can spread jealousy amongst its flock, and for some cunts the temptation to take what others have becomes too much. The modern day thefticunt is found in all countries, with varying concentrations. Israel, Australia and New Zealand currently have the highest rate of thefticunts per thousand cunts.

LIFE SPAN

Thefticunts don't tend to live long lives. Stealing can become a perpetual habit and their main natural predator is the policicunt. The vigilanticunt also targets them and has been known to kill if a thefticunt steps onto their property without permission.

SUB-BREEDS

**Carjackunt   Forgicunt   Fraudicunt
Muggicunt   Robbicunt**

HABITAT

The lifestyle of a thefticunt is not conducive to a stable habitat, and they usually live in cheap rented accommodation for short periods of time. Outside of their homes they lurk wherever large crowds form.

BEHAVIOUR

Thefticunts are edgy, jealous cunts. Always on the move, they are seemingly unable to relax and always hanker after stuff that isn't rightfully theirs. The more intelligent can be genius-like at times with their thought patterns in relation to taking stuff off others, excellent planners who studiously plot their next score. The less intelligent are altogether more basic cunts, and unsuccessfully attempt theft or leave trails that see them captured shortly after.

DIET

Thefticunts feed mostly on scraps. Their lifestyle is that of a cunt always on the move and food is therefore viewed as fuel.

REPRODUCTION

Thefticunts find it hard to commit to family scenarios due to the nature of their cuntishness, so don't breed in great numbers. When they do find themselves in a family environment they can be even more prolific, sometimes citing it as the only way they can provide for their families. Despite their low reproductive rates, numbers of thefitcunts are steadily on the rise the world over, maybe due to a widening gap between rich and poor.

The thefticunt is a master of disguise. Trainers and a weapon help them get in and out as quickly as possible

A bike fleeced of its assets by a thefticunt

Thrilsicunt

THE THRILLSEEKING CUNT

DESCRIPTION
The thrilsicunt is a physically capable broad-shouldered creature. These cunts often bear battlescars from their pursuits, with scratches, bruises and broken limbs regular features on their bodies. They usually dress practically rather than fashionably, and can be colourful cunts due to the demands of the pursuits they undertake. Thick fabrics are favoured, with protective headwear often accompanied by leather and synthetic rubber coated outfits.

DISTRIBUTION
The thrilsicunt seemed to originate in the 20th century, with the modern day beast favouring antipodean climes. Australia and New Zealand have the highest concentrations.

LIFE SPAN
Thrilsicunts have lower than average life spans. They take risks with their lives and favour short fun-fuelled lives to long boring ones. Their main predators come from the animal kingdom, with some thrilsicunts inevitably coming a cropper at the teeth of animals such as sharks and bears when cavorting in their habitats.

HABITAT
Thrilsicunts favour outdoor areas, often with little respect for the habitats of others. They find it hard to leave a settled existence and rarely nest in one location for any lengthy period of time.

BEHAVIOUR
All about adrenaline, thrilsicunts live their lives by the mantra that you only live once and usually believe their lives are fated. They are hyperactive and always up for a dare.

DIET
Thrilsicunts have a varied diet and will try anything that is put before them. This can include food, drink, or more challenging things they're dared to consume. Their pursuits are energetic so they will feast on calorific concoctions.

REPRODUCTION
Thrilsicunts can see children as a distraction to their spontaneous lifestyles and so aren't prolific breeders. Their numbers instead remain constant as they seem to form when trying to push pursuit-based boundaries in increasingly tech-led societies.

SUB-BREEDS

Activicunt   **Bunjicunt**   **Daredevicunt**   **Scubicunt**   **Stunticunt**

Afterword

The planet we inhabit is a beautiful one, but the natural evolution of humanity is now such that it is spawning new breeds of cunt at an alarming rate. These cunts are a scourge upon the Earth we populate, and, whilst the conundrum remains as to whether we should interfere in what technically is a natural phenomenon, if we could quickly identify what type of cunt we are encountering we could then modify our behaviour accordingly in order to avoid conflict and danger. A cowardicunt would know never to approach an aggressicunt, a capicunt would know to be wary of their fellow capicunt.

We must remain vigilant at all times and look out for those tell-tale cuntiqualities exhibited by each breed of cunt. We must all become cuntspotters for the sake of our brothers and our neighbours. If you encounter any new breeds of cunt then please share using the hashtag **#thebigbookofcunts**. It might just help us stave off this threat to humanity and help us all live happily together, side by side, forevermore.

Lightning Source UK Ltd.
Milton Keynes UK
UKOW07f0851041217
313843UK00008B/508/P